Betsy's Philadelphia Adventure

Coloring and Activity Book

Authors: Marcia Sawyer and Sandy Mayer

Illustrated by Milena and Jelena Vitorović

iPub Global Connection, LLC
1050 W. Nido Avenue
Mesa, AZ 85210
www.iPubCloud.com info@iPubCloud.com
US telephone: 484-775-0008

All rights reserved. Copyright © 2019 Marcia Sawyer and Sandy Mayer

No part of this book may be reproduced in any way without the express written permission of the publisher.

The views, opinions, and research expressed in this website/book are those of the authors and do not necessarily reflect the position of iPub Global Connection LLC.

Other iPub Global Connection books may be found at
https://www.iPubCloud.com

To Our Readers

We hope you have as much fun with this Coloring and Activity Book as we did creating it.

Below is the colonial flag featured at the Betsy Ross House.

a. How many stars are on the flag? _____
b. How many stripes are on the flag? _____

Betsy waves to Matthew across the street. He's an owner of Humphrys Flag Company where they make American flags.

"Benji invited me to a party at his new home," Betsy says to Matthew. "This invitation is a puzzle. I need to find his new home based on clues. It says that there's brick, a statue, and a game nearby. And his home is somehow related to Benjamin Franklin."

"Why don't you head up to the Benjamin Franklin Parkway, home to 109 flags from around the world? That street is named after Ben Franklin and I believe there's brick and sculpture nearby," suggests Matthew.

Below is the official United States flag used today.

a. How many stars are on the flag? _____
b. How many stripes are on the flag? _____

While on her way, Betsy spots a big brick building on South 3rd Street.

"YES, that must be Benji's house! He said it was brick!" Betsy says as she runs inside.

"Look! There's a tree in here!" says Betsy as she scampers to the top.

Looking down, she hears a guide tell visitors that the tree is the Boston Liberty Tree, where the founders of the U.S. planned the American Revolution.

"No, this is *not* Benji's new home," Betsy says as she runs outside and climbs the cannons in front of the building to look for new clues.

Circle the clues below that you saw mentioned on the previous pages that will be helpful to Betsy in solving this puzzle:

Bricks
Sculpture
Benjamin Franklin
Game/Place to Play

Draw a picture of each clue you circled.

Benji, Benji, where are you? wonders Betsy.

"Are you lost?" asks Stella, a beautiful great horned owl perched in a tree. "I am wise. I can help you find your way."

"I need to find my friend Benji's home," replies Betsy.

"Let's head down to 6th and Lombard," says the owl, pointing with his beak, "home to the Mother Bethel A.M.E. Church. It has lots of brick. Maybe Benji's party is there. I'll show you where it is."

When Betsy spots the red brick and white stone church, she climbs up the side of the building. She looks inside the empty church and says, "No, this is *not* Benji's new home."

"It may not be Benji's home, but it is home to an interesting museum in the basement," says Stella.

Circle the clues below that you saw mentioned on the previous pages that will be helpful to Betsy in solving this puzzle:

Bricks
Sculpture
Benjamin Franklin
Game/Place to Play

Draw a picture of each clue you circled.

Betsy zigzags down the block. She spies an old metal bell with brick buildings nearby.

"Let me see if I can spot Benji or his new home."

She notices the big crack down the middle of the bell, but no sign of Benji.

"No, this is *not* Benji's new home," she says.

A little pigeon agrees, "No this is *not* Benji's new home. But it is home to the 2,000 pound Liberty Bell. The bell rang in Independence Hall to announce the first reading of the Declaration of Independence."

Circle the clues below that you saw mentioned on the previous pages that will be helpful to Betsy in solving this puzzle:

- Bricks
- Sculpture
- Benjamin Franklin
- Game/Place to Play

Draw a picture of each clue you circled.

"I have an idea!" Betsy bursts out as she skitters past Insomnia Cookies and City Hall while heading toward Vine Street . "I'll look for the statue that Benji said is near his new home."

Betsy sees a big L-O-V-E statue and a blue fountain spouting behind it. "There it is! Maybe this is Benji's home?!"

She asks a friendly cheesesteak vendor, "Is this Benji the gray squirrel's new home?"

"No, this is *not* Benji's home. You're in LOVE Park. Check out the fun things to do here...ping-pong, big blocks, and other games. There's even a fountain. Feel free to jump in!"

Circle the clues below that you saw mentioned on the previous pages that will be helpful to Betsy in solving this puzzle:

Bricks
Sculpture
Benjamin Franklin
Game/Place to Play

Draw a picture of each clue you circled.

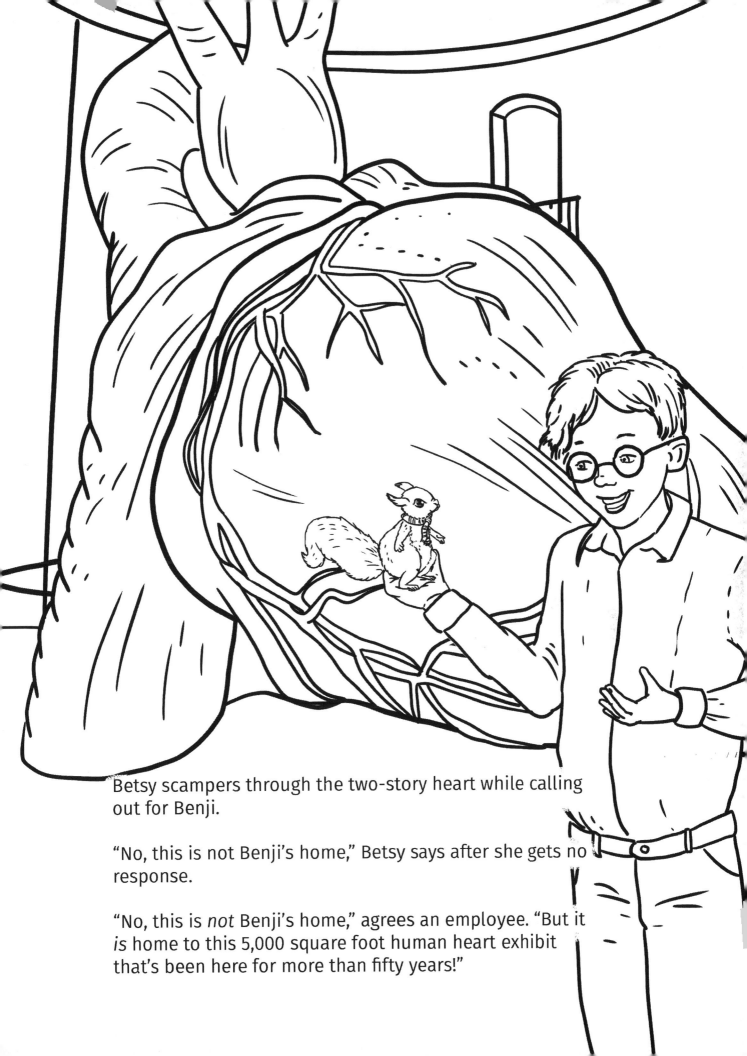

Betsy scampers through the two-story heart while calling out for Benji.

"No, this is not Benji's home," Betsy says after she gets no response.

"No, this is *not* Benji's home," agrees an employee. "But it *is* home to this 5,000 square foot human heart exhibit that's been here for more than fifty years!"

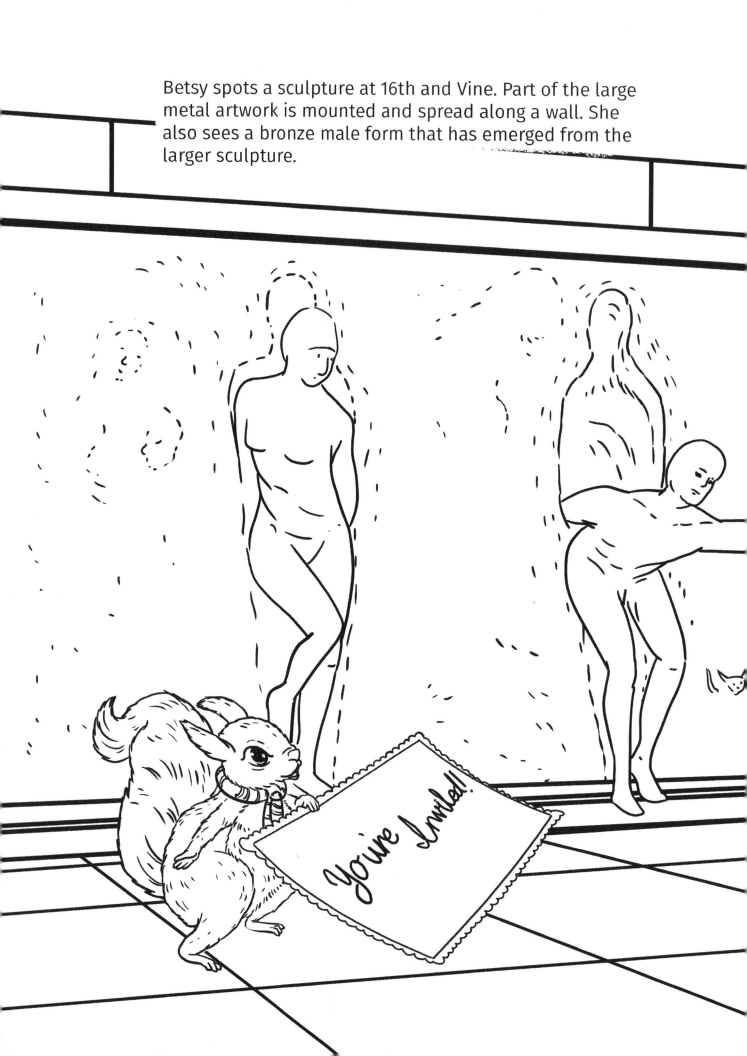

She asks a boy posing for a photo with the figure, "Is this Benji's new home? I am going to a party there."

"No, it's not. This is the Freedom sculpture which was created by Zenos Frudakis. Maybe you should head up toward Callowhill Street because there are a lot of people up that way. You might find your friend's party there...and yummy brick oven pizza," says the boy.

"Freedom" Copyright 2000 © Zenos Frudakis, sculptor

Circle the clues below that you saw mentioned on the previous pages that will be helpful to Betsy in solving this puzzle:

Bricks
Sculpture
Benjamin Franklin
Game/Place to Play

Draw a picture of each clue you circled.

Betsy smells something delicious as she approaches a crowd in front of Pizzeria Vetri on Callowhill Street. Then she sees Benji's friend Tug, an adorable pug dog. "Tug, is *this* Benji's new home? Is he having his party here?"

"No, this is *not* Benji's new home," says Tug. "But it *is* home to some of the best brick oven pizza in Philadelphia. I heard the Pizzeria Vetri food truck is at a party on Locust Walk in West Philadelphia."

"Maybe that's where Benji's party is," says Betsy.

"Let's go!" says Tug.

Circle the clues below that you saw mentioned on the previous pages that will be helpful to Betsy in solving this puzzle:

Bricks
Sculpture
Benjamin Franklin
Game/Place to Play

Draw a picture of each clue you circled.

Betsy and Tug walk down the brick Locust Walk at the University of Pennsylvania. Betsy sees another L-O-V-E sculpture.

Tug points to a sign, "Look, there's a football game that starts at 1 p.m. at Franklin Field."

"These things are all clues in the invitation. This must be Benji's party!" cheers Betsy.

"BENJI!" Betsy and Tug shout as they run towards Benji.

"YAY! You solved the puzzle!" says Benji.

"Is this your party, Benji?" asks Tug. "You have so many friends here!"

"Actually, Tug, this is the University of Pennsylvania's Homecoming party," says Benji. "It happens every year for students who have graduated from here. I invited you and my family and friends here to Penn's Homecoming because it's so much fun. And the Penn campus is now my new home."

CREDIT: © 2019 Morgan Art Foundation Ltd/ Artists Rights Society (ARS), NY

Circle the clues below that you saw on the previous pages that were helpful for Betsy in solving this puzzle:

Bricks
Sculpture
Benjamin Franklin
Game/Place to Play

Draw a picture of each clue you circled.

The friends munch on Philly favorites—cheesesteaks, Tastykakes®, and hot pretzels.

Draw a picture below of your favorite food!

Word Scramble

Unscramble the words:
1. lidehaPlihap
2. eysBt ssRo
3. retLbiy leBl
4. Tgu het gpu
5. neB kralnnFi
6. iserrluq
7. culpusert
8. ltfaoolb geam
9. ytarp
10. omsnlina okCoesi
11. ocmhnoegim
12. thsekceesea

squirrel	Betsy Ross	Liberty Bell
Tug the pug	party	homecoming
football game	cheesesteak	Ben Franklin
sculpture	Philadelphia	Insomnia Cookies

Word Search

A	E	S	M	B	H	E	E	L	E	L	P	L	L	
M	H	S	E	A	A	C	E	M	N	L	E	K	A	
A	O	C	K	Y	T	S	S	A	A	A	K	A	M	
L	M	K	A	T	O	P	L	L	M	H	L	E	B	
L	E	T	K	E	G	K	O	S	T	Y	I	T	B	
O	C	Z	Y	T	E	M	V	D	I	T	L	S	E	
C	O	T	T	B	E	P	E	N	H	I	K	E	T	
U	M	T	S	E	I	N	P	A	W	C	O	S	S	
S	I	N	A	T	R	M	A	B	T	A	M	E	Y	
T	N	D	T	P	H	P	R	T	L	A	S	E	R	
W	G	O	P	V	A	A	K	T	A	K	E	H	O	
A	N	H	K	P	H	E	E	U	W	E	E	C	S	
L	P	H	I	L	A	D	E	L	P	H	I	A	S	
K	T	I	S	S	U	P	V	B	A	H	S	E	M	

CITY HALL
PHILADELPHIA
PRETZEL
BETSY ROSS
BLUTT BAND SLAM
WALT WHITMAN

HOMECOMING
CHEESESTEAK
LOCUST WALK
TASTYKAKE™
LOVE PARK

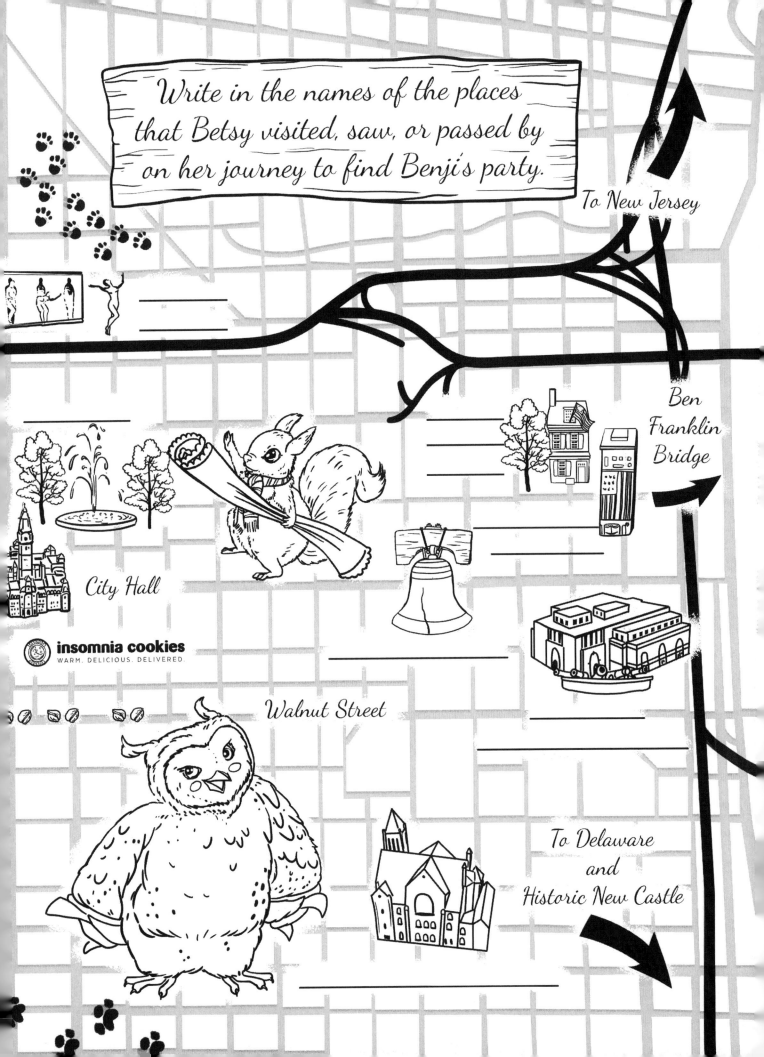

Made in the USA
Middletown, DE
28 June 2021